Sleep is for

Emily McDowall

Illustrated by Julia Hegetusch

SCHOLASTIC

SYDNEY AUCKLAND NEW YORK TORONTO LONDON MEXICO CITY
NEW DELHI HONG KONG BUENOS AIRES PUERTO RICO

For Mum and Dad, with love ~ Emily

For my Dad, Rolf Hegetusch ~ Julia

First published in 2024 by Scholastic New Zealand Limited
Private Bag 94407, Botany, Auckland 2163, New Zealand

Scholastic Australia Pty Limited
PO Box 579, Gosford, NSW 2250, Australia

ISBN 978-1-77543-843-4

A catalogue record for this book is available from the National Library of New Zealand.

---

12 11 10 9 8 7 6 5 4 3 2 1 4 5 6 7 8 9/2

Publishing team: Lynette Evans, Penny Scown and Abby Haverkamp
Designer: Vida Kelly
Typeset in Etna Regular
Printed in China by RR Donnelley

Scholastic New Zealand's policy is to use papers that are renewable and made efficiently from wood grown in responsibly managed forests, so as to minimise its environmental footprint.

"Good night," said the father.
"Now don't make a peep!"

But mischievous George
did **not** want to sleep.

Sleep is for babies!
he thought. *Not for me!*

There's too much to do
and too much to see.

So under the light

of a silvery moon,

rascally George

crept out of his room.

He swung open the door,
stepped into the night,
and startled the cat . . .
her back arched in fright!

“Come play with me, Cat!”
George got down on all fours.
“Let’s pretend to be lions . . .
but please don’t use claws.”

“The sun has long set,”
the puzzled cat said.
“Shouldn’t all children
be tucked up in bed?”

“Sleep is for babies!”
laughed George. “Not for me!”

So they jumped out at moths
and prowled round a tall tree.

Then the cat ran away
in pursuit of a mouse,
leaving George to explore
the bush past the house.

He heard a loud crashing
up in a tree top,
then down to the ground
a possum did drop!

"Come play with me, Possum,"
begged George. "Pretty please?
We can play statues
under the trees."

"You should be asleep!"
the possum growled back.
"I've no time for games,
but I *would* like a snack."

"Sleep is for babies!"
scoffed George. "Not for me!"
He showered the possum
with leaves from the tree.

But the possum got tired
of life on the ground,
and he climbed up the tree,
yelling, “See you around!”

George pushed through some flax,
and there on a log,
croaking contentedly,
sat a green frog.

"Come play with me, Frog!
We can make funny faces,
take turns at hopscotch
and have lily-pad races."

“It’s late for a little one,”
said the frog with a frown.
“Shouldn’t you sleep
in your own part of town?”

“Sleep is for babies!”
said George with some pride.
“I bet I could stay up
all night if I tried!”

The frog and the boy
bounced high in the air,
till the frog found a friend
and both frogs disappeared.

Alone in the dark,
George felt ready to cry,
but just then an owl
swooped down from the sky.

George's voice trembled
as he started to speak,
"Will you play with me, Ruru?
Perhaps hide-and-seek?"

"A night owl!" laughed Ruru,
her eyes big and wide.
"Very well then, I'll count
and you go off and hide."

George discovered a tree
with a hollow his size,
then gathered up ferns
to make a disguise.

"Coming, ready or not!"
he heard Ruru call.
George curled himself into
a tight little ball.

As he lay in the ferns,
all snuggly and cosy,

our brave little George
began to feel dozy.

His head felt all heavy,
his breathing soon slowed,

and just as his eyelids
got droopy and closed . . .

"Found you!" screeched Ruru
right next to his ear,
and then, more severely,
"You look *tired*, my dear.

"It is high time for you
to get a good rest.
The glowworms will help light
the way to your nest."

So George found his way
through the trees to the lawn,
and into the house
as he stifled a yawn.

"Sleep is for babies,"
George murmured. "It's boring.
Sleep – is – for . . ."

Next thing, he was snoring.